First published in Great Britain in 2017 by Andersen Pre

20 Vauxhall Bridge Road, London SW1V 2SA.

Copyright © Tony Ross, 2017.

The rights of Tony Ross to be identified as the author

illustrator of this work have been asserted by him in acc

with the Copyright, Designs and Patents Act, 198

All rights reserved.

Colour separated in Switzerland by Photolitho AG Zü

Printed and bound in China.

1   3   5   7   9   10   8   6   4

British Library Cataloguing in Publication Data avai

ISBN 978 1 78344 493 9

# OUR KID

## Tony Ross

Andersen Press

Our Kid was late for school again.

He didn't have his homework or his uniform either, so his teacher sent him straight to the Naughty Corner.

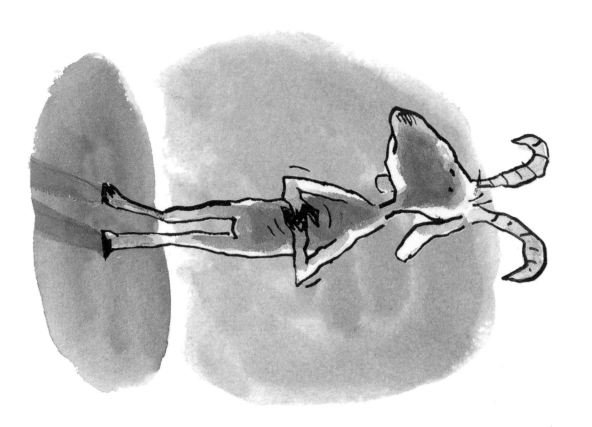

"Please, Sir," squeaked Our Kid.
"I left on time this morning
and my mum said,
'Remember to take
your homework.'

And my dad said, 'Go straightly to school,
Our Kid. Don't be late again.'

So I shoffled my homework into my
bag and took the shortcut.

When you take the shortcut along the beach, you have to dunkle your hooves in the water.

Suddenly a submarine splooshed up out of the waves and squeaked across the sand.

sploosh!

Peeping in a porthole, I saw it was full of water.
And the water was full of fish.

Their leader, Captain Mackerel,
said that they were chasing pirates and
could take me to school on the way.

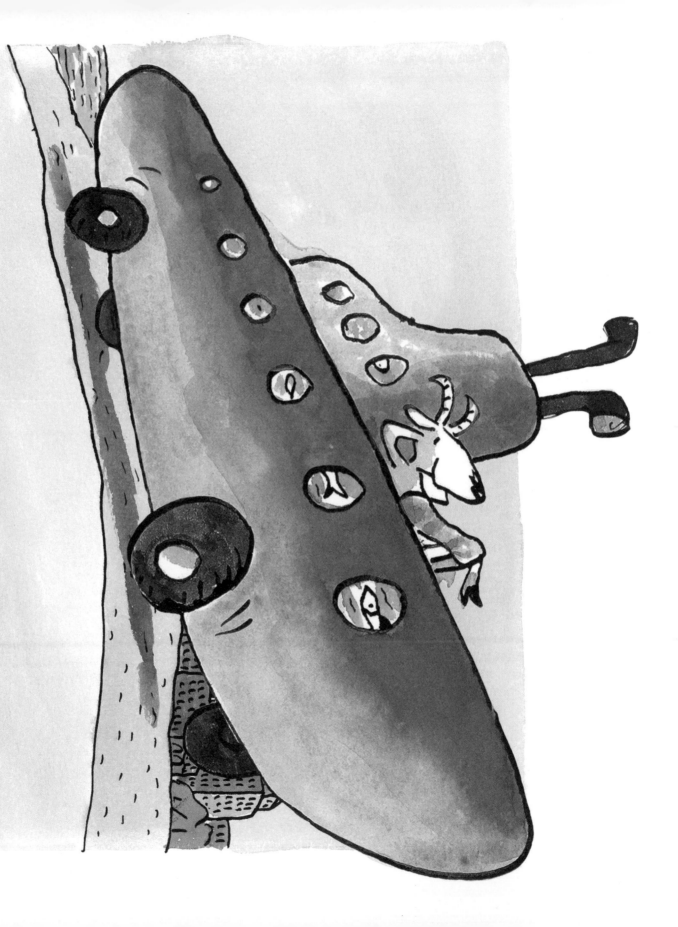

As it was too watery inside the submarine, I rode on the deck, and off we **bumpeeded** down the road. But before the fish could find the pirates…

... the pirates found the fish!

These were dinopirates, so some were squiddly, but others were felumpingly big.

The big ones shook the submarine.

The fish were safe
inside, but I fell
into the pirates'
clutches.

They snitched
my trousers and
my schoolbag.

"My homework's in that!"
I cried, as the
pirates sniggled and
bounded away.

I tried to stop them, but they were too big.
And if I had, they probably would've eaten me.

"Hello!"
boomdered a voice.

An elephant had
snuck up behind me.
He was not a wild
elephant, because
he was wearing a
belt and a shed on
his back.
He asked me, 'Why
so glumbumtious,
little goat?'

I told him how late I was for school, so he offered me a lift, high up on his back.

Which was lucky, because it was a long way over the **craggly** mountains and across the wide blue water. And I got to see it all, without getting **snarked** by crocodiles.

snap

snark

snap

When we got to school I said thank you
and the elephant *kerlumped* away.

And that's why I got here so late,
without my homework or my trousers."

"Our Kid, be hushled!" cried the teacher.

"Children, what do we call someone who makes up such total and utter nonsense?"

A good goat is on time, does their homework and never lies.

But just then...

# Kerumble!

The school began to shake.

Desks tipped over and chairs bounced around as everybody scrambled out of the nearest window or door.

But Our Kid wasn't allowed to leave the Naughty Corner... so he was still there when three aliens walked in!

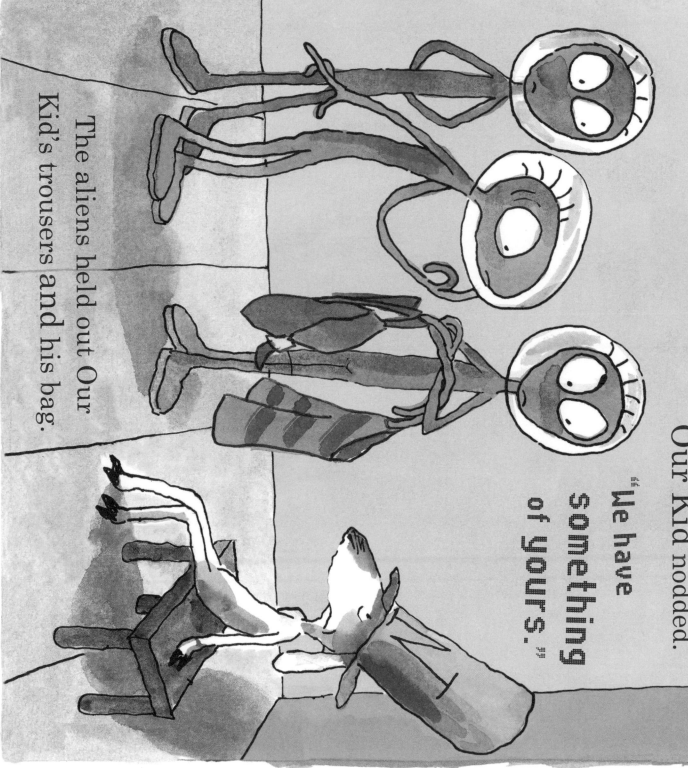

"Are you Our Kid?" asked the aliens.

Our Kid nodded.

"We have something of yours."

The aliens held out Our Kid's trousers and his bag.

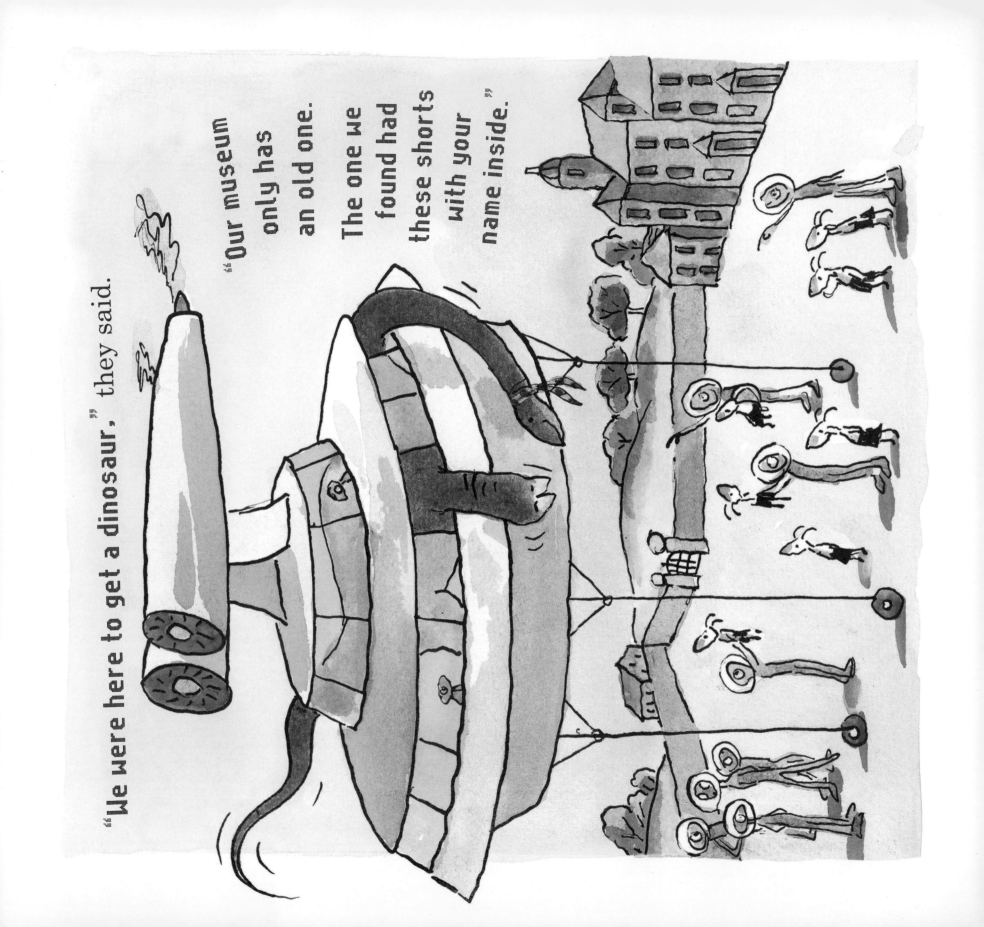

"We were here to get a dinosaur," they said.

"Our museum only has an old one.

The one we found had these shorts with your name inside."

The dinopirate was excited to be visiting a new planet and the whole class waved goodbye as the spaceship zerumbled off.

Then everyone ran back inside.

"You were **bravey** to face the aliens like that," said his teacher.

Our Kid handed in his homework and the teacher gave him a gold star and an apple, without even reading it.

"You can be as late as you like tomorrow," he chuckled.

This time Our Kid skipped straightly home, with no shortcuts and his head full of adventures.

"You're back early," said his mum.
"So, what happened today?" asked his dad.

"Nuffin," said Our Kid.